Dedicated to:

My Mama—You are my biggest fan! You've loved Dusternuffle from the moment it was first created, more than anyone. You not only believed in this book, but you believe in me, breathing life into my dreams. Thank you for all the bedtime stories, the Barbie playdates, the Andy Griffith lunches, the Mary Harry moments, lunch notes and Landlord letters. You are the best mother and friend. I love you more than mostest!
Forever my Lucy, Always your Ethel!
-Rebecca

London, Clara, Corin, and Oliver my 4 crazy dusty little people.
You fill my life with beautiful messy magic and will be my inspiration forever.
I love you to the moon and back.
-Cassi
-

Dusternuffle
Text Copyright ©2020 by Rebecca Greenfield
Illustrations Copyright ©2020 by Cassandra Zook

Library of Congress Cataloging-in-Publication Data
Library of Congress Control Number: 2020919533
Greenfield, Rebecca
        Dusternuffle / Rebecca Greenfield
                p. cm.
        ISBN: 978-0-578-77936-2

1st Printing. Printed in Columbus, OH

DUSTERNUFFLE

REBECCA GREENFIELD & CASSANDRA ZOOK

Underneath the rooftop and below the furniture

laid a small village called Dusternuffle. Dusternuffle was located in the carpet of the Tamber family house. In the quaint village of Dusternuffle, all the Dustanians in their little dust bodies and their little dust homes lived in peace and happiness, including the Puffdust family. Each Tamber family day was a year to the Dustanians. Everyday Mr. Puffdust went to work while Mrs. Puffdust dirtied up the house, instead of cleaned it, and sent Dusty and Dirty off to school.

Mr. Puffdust

Mrs. Puffdust

Dirty

Dusty

The Puffdust Family was dearly loved in the village of Dusternuffle. Mr. Puffdust was one of the best workers at the local Ant Mill. He could package up crumbs in record time. He was speedier than an ant and even won the Crumbleton Award for dustiest achievement. Oh and Mrs. Puffdust...she was treasured by all! She was always helping the dustless, often giving crumbs to those in need. She hustled and bustled but never forgot to spread the dust. And little Dusty and Dirty? Why, they were just as lovable and dustable as their parents! They shared their savory soot stained sandwiches at school and played grubby games with their friends at recess. God had dusted the Puffdust family and so they made every effort to dust others.

Just like everyone in Dusternuffle, the Puffdust family celebrated traditions and holidays by going to ant parades and beetle festivals. Sometimes the Puffdust family would pack up and leave their country of Carpeto to take a vacation to the country of Dirtland. But the Puffdust family had also experienced sadness. About every 7 years, in Dusternuffle time, a tornado (which was actually Mrs. Tamber sweeping the house) swept through their beautiful village. And every so often there would be humanquakes, when little Tommy Tamber jumped on the carpet. But the humanquakes and the tornadoes weren't nearly as bad as the 30 year hurricane, (which was when the Tamber family had their carpet shampooed once a month).

In the last 30 year hurricane, nearly the whole country of Carpeto was washed away, all except Mayor Dustford, and Mrs. Spider-Ider, who was left a black widow from the hurricane. A few other families survived here and there, but they were the very wisest in the village.

Mayor Dustford called a village meeting to warn all the Dustanians about the upcoming 30 year hurricane.

"Welcome Dustanians.

I have called this village meeting to come up with a plan
to stop the 30 year hurricane. Any ideas?"

"Well, we could all pack up and go to Dirtland,"
Mrs. Spider-Ider said from her web.

"But our precious hand-dusted
houses will be destroyed,"
replied Mayor Dustford.

"Maybe we could make it extra dusty all over so that the hurricane can't
get through," said another Dustanian.

"No, we don't have enough time to make that
much extra dust," the Mayor answered.

"Any other suggestions?"

All the Dustanians were silent because
they were thinking hard how to save their village.

Suddenly, Mr. Puffdust blurted out in pure excitement,
"Why don't we have Mrs. Spider-Ider make a protective web over our
town of Dusternuffle? Her web is sticky and waterproof so it will
protect us from all the hurricane's rain."

"Well, Mr. Puffdust," Mayor Dustford replied,
"I don't know. That's a risky idea, but yet a mighty fine one. What do
the rest of you Dustanians think?"

"Sound's good to me," said one Dustanian.
"Sounds good to me, too," replied another.
"Well, I think it is a great idea," said another.

The whole town hoorayed with great joy.

"Would you be willing to help us, Mrs. Spider-Ider?" asked the Mayor.
"I would be most honored," answered Mrs. Spider-Ider, "and I will ask
President Daddy Long Legs and Vice President Richard Recluse of the Red
Pine Cross to help me spin. I'll even ask the spinsters from the Pinewood
church to come! I know our neighbors from Pinewood would all love to help."

"Good then, we'll start tomorrow. Mr. Puffdust, since this was your idea, I am going to put you in charge of this plan. Please come with Mrs. Spider-Ider and inform us what to do." Mrs. Spider-Ider told Mr. Puffdust what to say.

"Alright everyone, I need a crew to direct the Pinewoodians in from the north. I need a crew for the south, and a crew for the east and west." All the Dustanians huddled together and then divided into groups. Mrs. Spider-Ider quickly left to go visit Pinewood and ask them for their much needed help.

As darkness fell over the tiny town of Dusternuffle, all the Dustanians began to take their positions to the north, south, east and west. All the dust factories and ant mills shut down. Some Dustanians who weren't able to help in the web-making mission went to the Dusternuffle Town Church to pray that God would stop the hurricane. Mrs. Puffdust gathered all the Dustanian ladies to ask them to bake fly-pie potatoes and dirt-fried stew for the Pinewoodians who would be working so hard.

Soon the town
of Pinewood
came crawling in
from all directions. The country
of Carpeto was being covered by
spiders great and small.

"I think the plan is working," said Mr. Puffdust to Mayor Dustford.
"I think so, too," said the Mayor excitedly.

Spider after spider kept crawling in—some with their friends, some with their husbands, and some with their wives and children too. Time was flying by with each spider that continued to enter Carpeto. The whole town and country was getting covered with a huge, beautiful web with barely an hour to spare.

All the Dustanians went back to their little dust homes and waited for the 30 year hurricane. Mr. and Mrs. Puffdust tucked Dusty and Dirty into their beds.

"Mom, do you think the hurricane will come?" asked Dusty.
"I'm scared," said Dirty.

"Well, dears, I don't know if the hurricane will come or not. You just keep praying and God will protect us," Mrs. Puffdust said tenderly.

The whole town of Dusternuffle settled down to go to bed. The Tamber family was moving furniture as they prepared to shampoo the carpet and the thunderous thuds made the Dustanians shudder.

The rain began to pour and the wind began to howl.

All the Dustanians hoped and prayed to wake up and find their village still there and not washed away. Dusty and Dirty prayed in their beds.

"Dear God, please dust our town.
Web us safe from the hurricane. Amen."

The next morning as the Dustanians awoke from their dreams, Mr. and Mrs. Puffdust opened their front door and much to their surprise, their whole village was there. The hurricane didn't harm the village of Dusternuffle.

That day the village of Dusternuffle had a
big festival and celebrated by eating dusterberry pie
and critter custard cake. Mayor Dustford spoke,
"This is the first time in the history of Dusternuffle that we have
survived the 30 year hurricane! God has saved us! We did it—all of us
together!" "Hooray," shouted all the Dustanians and Pinewoodians.

"Mr. Puffdust, we would like you to be the Village Manager of Dusternuffle.
"Hooray," shouted everybody. "And, Mrs. Spider-Ider we would like you
to be the President of Carpeto." "Hooray," yelled the Dustanians and
Pinewoodians.

The whole village of Dusternuffle clapped in cheer. On they went, surviving one hurricane after another with the help of their 8-legged friends. Never had the village of Dusternuffle enjoyed life as much as they did after defeating the 30 year hurricane for the first time.

THE DUSTERNUFFLE GOSPEL

Dusty and Dirty knew that if they prayed, God would watch over them. Sometimes life can get scary, but God loves you and wants you to know He is always with you. Even when bad things happen you can trust that God is bigger, stronger and never going to leave you. You can always talk to God no matter where you are or what is happening. He always hears you, just like He heard the Dustanians.

Did you know that God loves you so much He wants you to live with Him forever in Heaven? But God is so perfect that He can't have any bad things or sin in Heaven because it would upset Him too much. So do you know what God did to solve this problem? He sent His son Jesus from Heaven to Earth so that Jesus would remove all the bad things and sin away from people including you. *(If you want to learn even more about all Jesus did, you can read about it in your Bible in Matthew 26-28.)*

Every person that tells God they are sorry for the bad things they do and believes that He forgives them for their sins is washed clean. When God looks at them, they no longer look bad and sinful, they look perfect and clean, just like Jesus. But some people never tell God they are sorry or believe that Jesus loves them. This makes God sad because He loves everyone so much. He doesn't want anyone to go to a scary, hurtful, lonely place called Hell. It's a million times worse than the 30 year hurricane. Instead God wants you and everyone to be with Him in Heaven one day, safe from all bad things, rescued just like the town of Dusternuffle. Do you want to go to Heaven with God? If so, why don't you tell God?

Just say:

"Dear God, I am sorry for everything I did bad and will ever do bad. I don't want to do bad things anymore, but even if I do bad things accidentally, I pray you will forgive me. I believe you sent Jesus your son, to help me and wash away my sins. I believe you love me so much and that is why Jesus died on the cross and came back to life. One day I want to live with you in Heaven forever and ever. Thank you for hearing my prayer. Thank you for always being with me. I love you! In Jesus Name, Amen."

You know what? You just made God SO happy!

you are so loved!

MEET the
author and illustrator

REBECCA
GREENFIELD

REBECCA GREENFIELD is the author of RAW Inner Workings of a Reawakened Soul, RAW Reawakened Soul Study Guide, The Prayer Crossing Personal Devotional: A 28-Day Guide to Quality Time with God and The Prayer Crossing Event Workbook. After earning her bachelors in Nuclear Medicine Technology, she followed God's call into ministry and obtained her masters in Theological Studies. She is blessed to pursue both of her passions, science and theology, by working in nuclear medicine and at Lifeline Christian Mission. One of her deepest desires is to create spaces and places where people can experience the presence of God and be enveloped in His love. Aside from God, nothing brings her more joy than spending time with her wonderful husband, family, and friends.

Connect with Rebecca at
www.Rebecca-Greenfield.com

CASSANDRA
ZOOK

Cassandra Zook is an illustrator, surface designer, artist, wife, and mom to four beautiful unruly kids. Nestled in the rolling hills of rural northeastern Ohio, She fills her days creating patterns and illustrations and chasing around her almost preschooler. She finds inspiration in the world around her, her family, her faith, and in filling her home and imagination with books.

From the time she could hold a pencil she has been drawing and doodling on every scrap of paper available. After earning a degree in graphic design she and her husband got married and started a family. Throughout the last several years most of her creative work has been poured into her local church.

After homeschooling her children for 6 years she discovered a deep passion for cultivating truth, goodness, and beauty in the lives of others. Her hope is that through her work she can inspire others and reflect the love of the very first creator.

Connect with Cassandra at
www.cassandrazook.com

POOF

Book & Cover Design By: Cassandra Zook